Corson

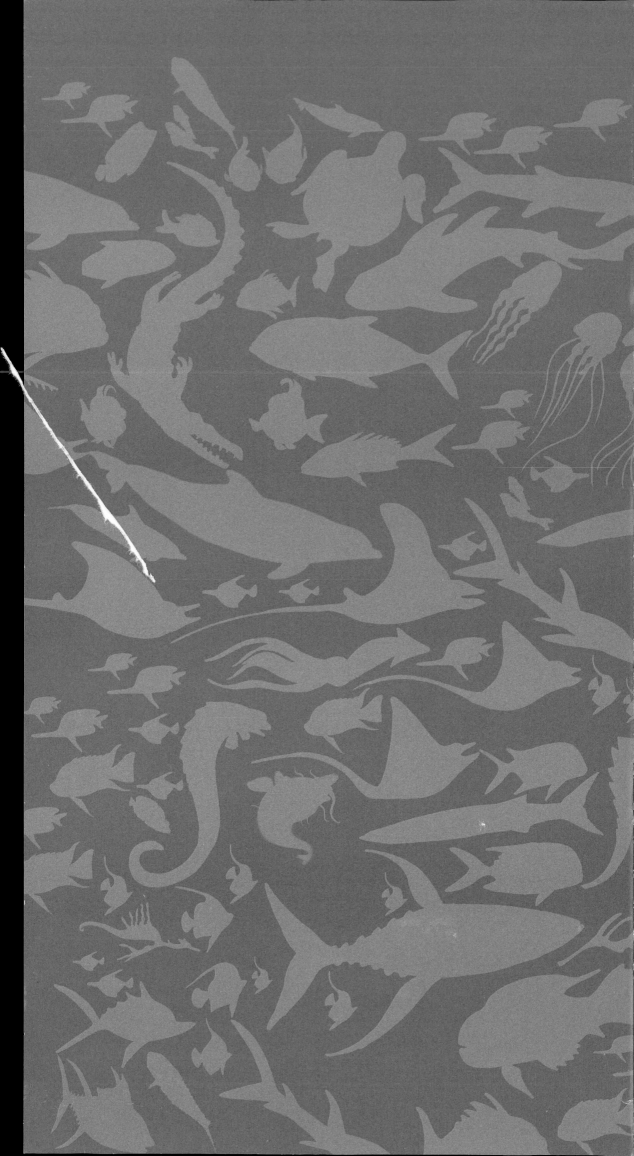

Fire Fish

fins refined by fire

DAVY LIU

KENDUFILMS
PRODUCTIONS

Written and illustrated
by Davy Liu

Grateful acknowledgement to Lynnette Baum for her creative input and insight.

Special thanks to my mother and father; my wife, Joan, my constant friend; Pastor Mike Fabarez; my manager Sabrina; Dr. Mark Arvidson; Sheila Tseng; Nancy Brashear; Gabrien and Rusan Symons; Holy Family Cathedral School; the support and prayers of my small group.

D.L.

© 2008 by Kendu Films, Inc. All rights reserved.

Published in the United States by Kendu Films, Inc.
3275K Laguna Canyon Road, Laguna Beach, CA 92651
www.kendufilms.com

Unless otherwise indicated, all Scriptures are taken from the Holy Bible, New International Version, Copyright 1973, 1978, 1984 by the International Bible Society. Used by permission of Zondervan Publishing House. The "NIV" and "New International Version" trademarks are registered in the United States Patent and Trademark Office by International Bible Society.

ISBN 978-0-615-19233-8

Printed in Taiwan.

For His Pleasure

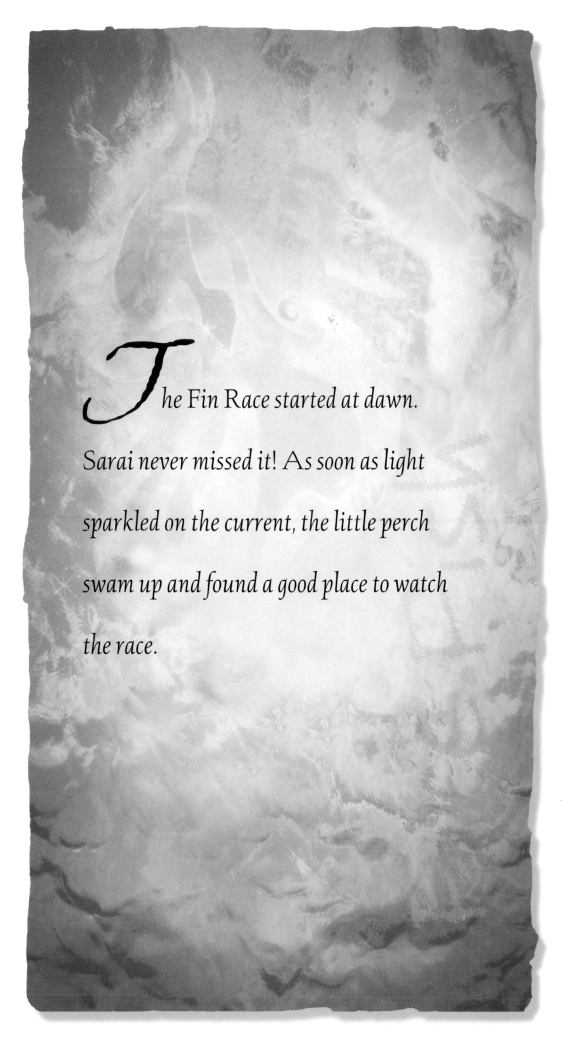

The Fin Race started at dawn.

Sarai never missed it! As soon as light

sparkled on the current, the little perch

swam up and found a good place to watch

the race.

The biggest, fastest, smartest fish always joined the Fin Race. Each day, a few won and caught the sweet lovely-food that came at sunrise. Then they disappeared into the Bright Beyond where all food was lovely-food.

"And best of all," thought Sarai, "any ordinary fish can be a Fire Fish in the Bright Beyond!"

With a sigh, Sarai watched as the last lovely-food was gobbled up. Slowly, she swam back down to her family.

"I w-wish we could race for l-lovely-food," stuttered Sesom, Sarai's shy little brother. "I'm hungry."

His tummy rumbled.

"We may not be the fastest swimmers," Momma Perch said, "but the Finmaker made us—"

"I know, I know. Steady swimmers!" RaaOn interrupted. He had heard this many times before.

"Look!" He pointed with his fin.

Pappa Perch had returned. He swam toward them, tugging strands of old green-blossom through the reeds.

"You children can eat first," said Momma Perch.

As Sarai nibbled, she thought of the legend she heard about the two-legged ones. They were once thrown into the current where crocs feasted on them. Mothers had wept on the bank, and river fish tasted their tears.

That's when the first Fire Fish was seen. It blazed across the Bright Beyond and picked up a young two-legged one who was hidden in an egg of reeds. Since then, it was rumored that when fish entered the Bright Beyond, they, too, turned into Fire Fish.

Sarai flipped her ordinary tail, "I want to be a Fire Fish!"

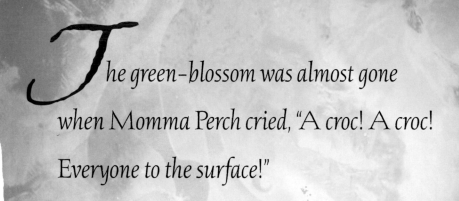

The green-blossom was almost gone when Momma Perch cried, "A croc! A croc! Everyone to the surface!"

They darted away from the crocs, unaware of the net above until it caught Momma and Pappa Perch.

"Nets aren't like lovely-food. You never know where they will take you," shouted Pappa Perch. "Go to the Turtle Pool and ask for help. We'll try to find you there!"

The little perch knew they had to find the Turtle Pool quickly. Darting from rock to rock, they swam upriver to a turtle-shaped pond behind a huge boulder.

"Thank the Finmaker! We made it," RaaOn gasped.

But the boulder shuddered, turned, and blocked the entrance. A rough head with pebble eyes popped out near the river bottom. The perch were trapped

"Why are you here?" asked a deep voice. It was the biggest turtle they had ever seen!

"Our parents were netted and sent us here to ask for help," Sarai said.

"Ah," nodded the Great Turtle wisely. "This is where calls are offered."

"Call on the Finmaker," he continued. "It is your only chance to find them again."

"D-do we have to call out l-loud?" Sesom asked.

"Call from your heart," the turtle said. "You will feel the answer, even if it is only, 'Be patient.'"

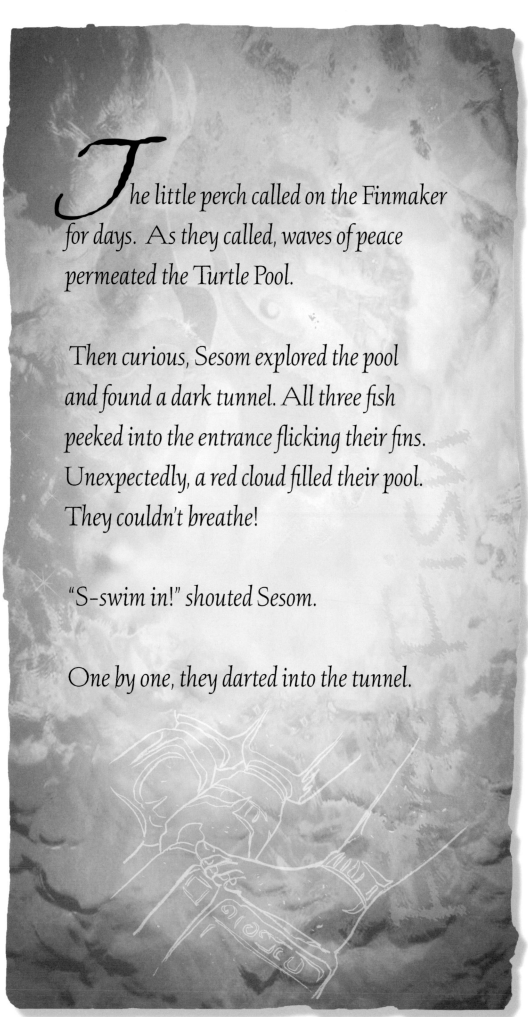

The little perch called on the Finmaker
for days. As they called, waves of peace
permeated the Turtle Pool.

Then curious, Sesom explored the pool
and found a dark tunnel. All three fish
peeked into the entrance flicking their fins.
Unexpectedly, a red cloud filled their pool.
They couldn't breathe!

"S-swim in!" shouted Sesom.

One by one, they darted into the tunnel.

They swam through the darkness.

"Here, a Fire Fish could light the way," Sarai thought.

Then, something gleamed. RaaOn and Sarai darted toward it.

"W-wait for me," Sesom cried.

"Yesss! Wait!" a voice hissed.

An eel swayed before them, eyes burning. "Come clossser. I will guide you to the Big Blue."

"W-what's the Big Blue?" asked Sesom.

"It's where currentsss are warm and green-blosssoms are sssweet!"

"I think we should call on the Finmaker instead!" said Sarai.

Immediately, a current swept them further down the cold, black tunnel. The eel's snout snapped after them, thrashing the water to foam.

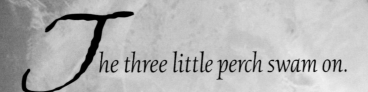

The three little perch swam on.

The darkness seemed endless. Moss, like slimy tentacles, combed their fins. Muddy water swirled and made it hard for them to breathe. Strange scraping and scuttling sounds frightened them. The only hope they had left was the thought of the Big Blue, a watery paradise.

Finally, tired and hungry, they trusted in the Finmaker's care and dreamed.

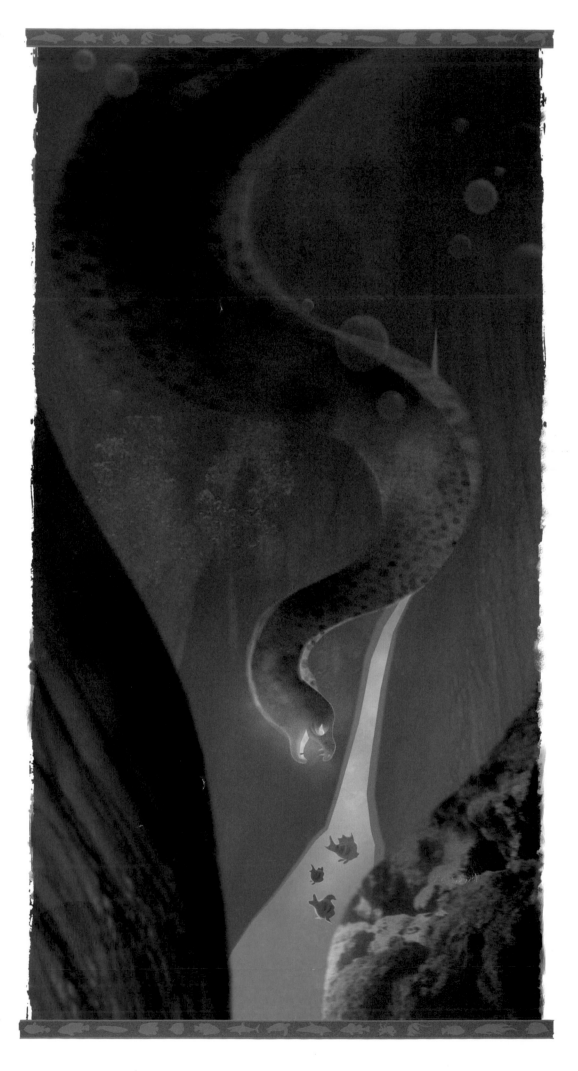

*B*ack at the entrance of the tunnel, the eel angrily lashed his tail.

"I am hungry," he growled, licking his fangs. "I must find those tasssty fish."

He chased after the perch through the tunnel with wicked speed, nosing into every crack and cave.

Meanwhile, the tired perch slept deeply. RaaOn dreamed of green-blossom. Sesom dreamed of sunny waters. As Sarai dreamed of the majestic Fire Fish, she suddenly blinked awake to see two glowing eyes streaming directly toward her.

"Swim!" she shouted.

Just in time, they darted out of the dangerous tunnel.

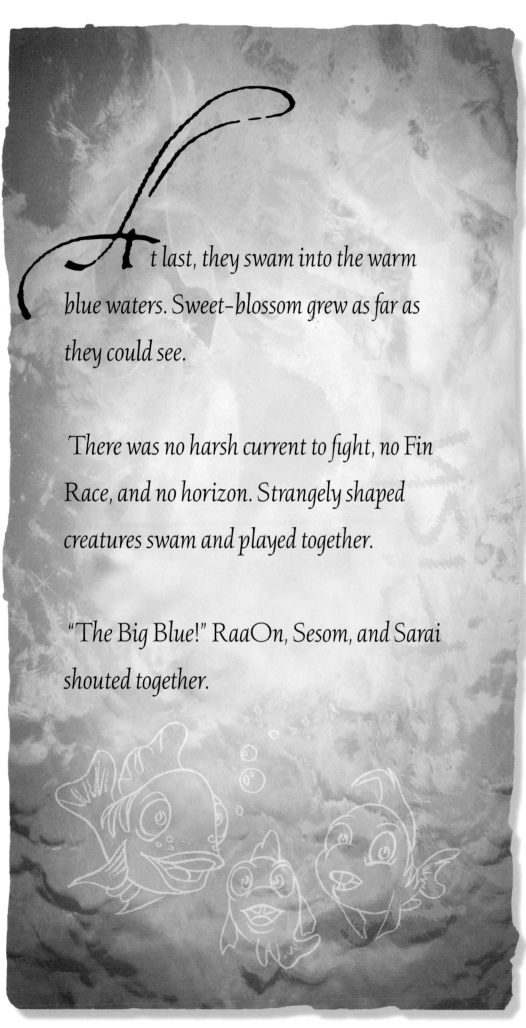

At last, they swam into the warm blue waters. Sweet-blossom grew as far as they could see.

There was no harsh current to fight, no Fin Race, and no horizon. Strangely shaped creatures swam and played together.

"The Big Blue!" RaaOn, Sesom, and Sarai shouted together.

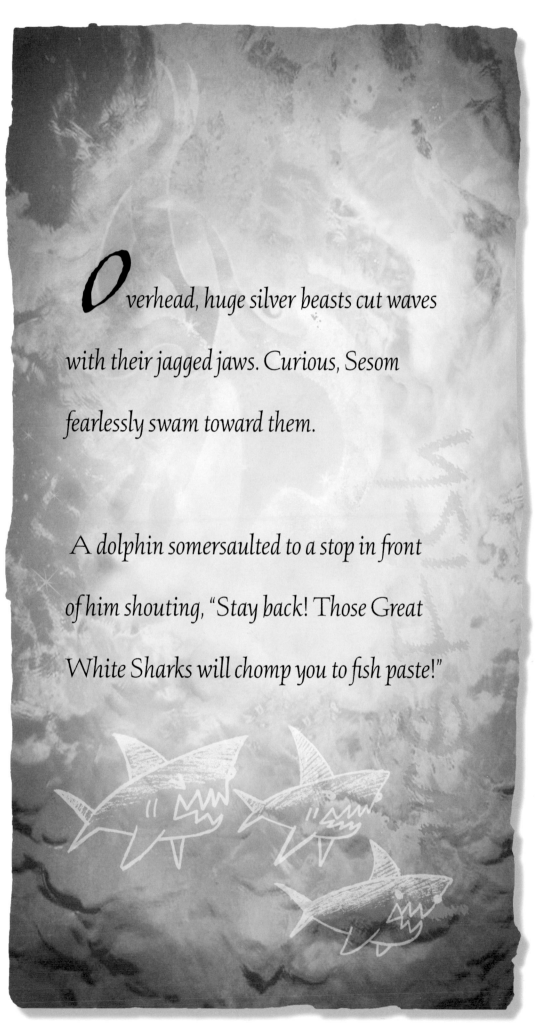

*O*verhead, huge silver beasts cut waves

with their jagged jaws. Curious, Sesom

fearlessly swam toward them.

A dolphin somersaulted to a stop in front

of him shouting, "Stay back! Those Great

White Sharks will chomp you to fish paste!"

The dolphin told them about the Big Blue and tales of the Great Whites, always hungry and hunting. She chattered stories of Purple Deeps, home to whales and giant squids. She sang fables of White Beaches, where starfish twirled and seahorses danced.

In return, the perch told her about the quest to find their parents.

"You're lucky to escape from that deceitful eel!" the dolphin said. "How did you do it?"

"We c-called on the Finmaker," replied Sesom.

"I don't know who this Finmaker is. Here, we call on ourselves," said the dolphin.

With a sound like stones skipping on water, a family of flying fish arched toward them.

"Killer is coming!" they squeaked and flipped away. Before Sarai, RaaOn, and Sesom could blink, the tuna had darted off in a glittering cloud while the octopus, crab, and stingray flicked into hiding places in the reef. Even the dolphin was gone.

"Where did everybody go?" RaaOn asked with a trembling voice.

"Blend in!" hissed a seahorse.

"Use magic," whispered a baby octopus, squirting a cloud of ink.

"Hide yourselves," growled a digging crab.

But it was too late! The three little perch were left alone in the Big Blue.

With a roar, Killer dove toward the perch with jaws open wide.

"Tag! You're it!" he shouted at them.

"It's about time you showed up to meet our new friends," the dolphin welcomed him. "Hiding from him is a game," she turned to wink at them. "He's a real killer!"

"No time for jokes," Killer boomed.

"You're all in danger!"

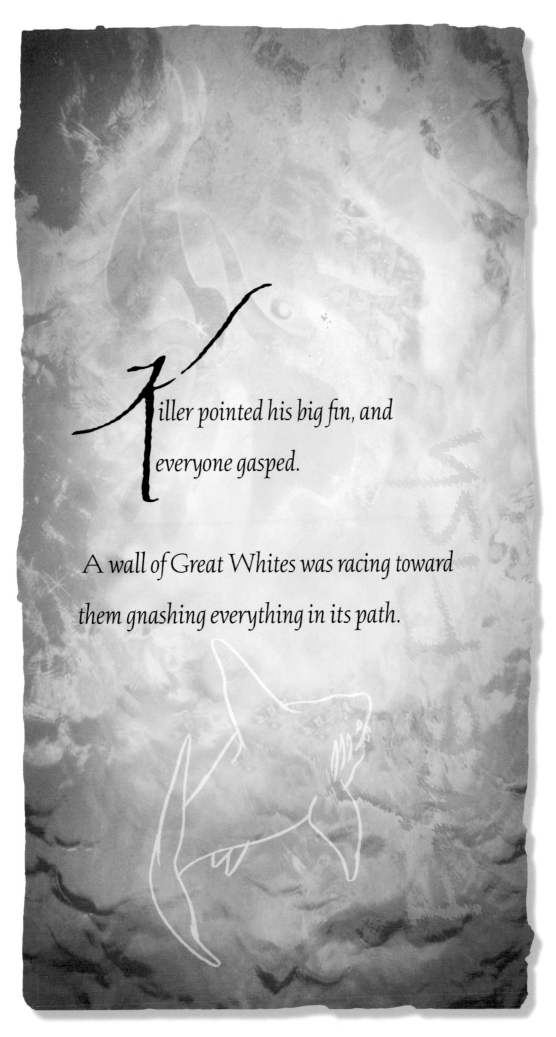

Killer pointed his big fin, and
everyone gasped.

A wall of Great Whites was racing toward
them gnashing everything in its path.

Tuna darted everywhere in panic. Seahorses buried themselves. An octopus fought with his brother over a coral cranny while stingrays flapped in fear. Big crabs stumbled over baby crabs in their hurry to hide. Sarai swam in front of her brothers protectively as if to fight the Great Whites off alone.

Sesom nosed a baby crab right side up and pushed it to safety.

"I kn-know what to do!" he cried.

Slowly, the sea creatures gathered around the little perch.

"We c-can't out swim them," Sesom said. "And, th-there aren't enough holes to hide everyone. We must c-call on the Finmaker for help!"

"That's your idea?" Killer scoffed. "If we stay still and call, they'll eat us!"

"We were safe in the Turtle Pool because we called," Sarai said.

"We escaped the black eel because we called," RaaOn said.

"He h-helped us then," Sesom said. "He will help us now!"

So the little perch called on the Finmaker, and the sea creatures stayed still, listening, too frightened to move.

*N*othing happened...

The cove creatures scuttled and scurried frantically for cover, too frightened to think of anyone but themselves. Tuna darted while the dolphins and Killer prepared for battle.

With Sarai on one side and RaaOn on the other, Sesom put his fins together and called out again.

"Oh, F-Finmaker, you helped us in the past, please put f-friendly fish on one side and enemy fish on the other!"

There was silence followed by a great roar, and the Big Blue parted.

Everyone stopped. Amazed, they gathered around the little perch.

"The Finmaker answered your call!" a stingray said.

"The F-Finmaker answers everyone who calls," Sesom replied.

Then, in a burst of glory, the Fire Fish appeared. They swam past in a shining river, as if the sun had shattered, scattering its brilliance in a current of stars between the friendly fish and their enemies. Their radiance touched each sea creature's heart and changed fear into faith.

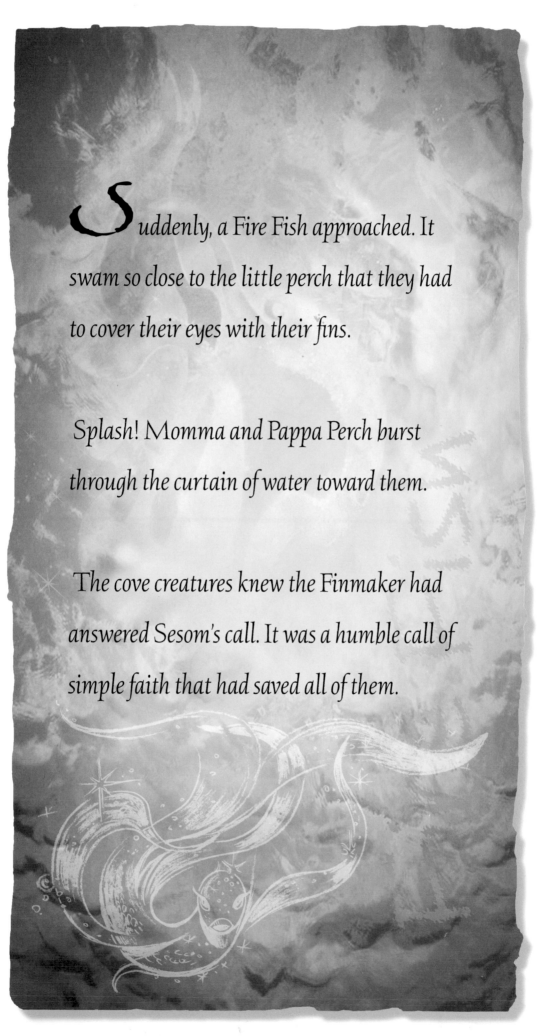

Suddenly, a Fire Fish approached. It swam so close to the little perch that they had to cover their eyes with their fins.

Splash! Momma and Pappa Perch burst through the curtain of water toward them.

The cove creatures knew the Finmaker had answered Sesom's call. It was a humble call of simple faith that had saved all of them.

"*I c-called, Momma, and the water moved,*" Sesom said proudly. The little perch and their parents nuzzled each other happily.

Sarai looked at her family, and her fins quivered with pride. The Fire Fish were special, but as long as she had family to love, she was special, too!

"Your call brought us a miracle," said the dolphin, speaking for all. "But what happens when the walls of water close up again? Won't the Great Whites eat us then?"

"*R*emember how the first Fire Fish saved the young two-legged one in the egg of reeds?" asked Momma Perch. "Well, a Fire Fish and a young two-legged one kept us in an egg of clay, too."

"The two-legged ones made us pets," Pappa Perch added. "And gave us fresh river water every day."

"We watched and learned how the Fire Fish led the way through the darkness, so that the two-legged could escape from angry enemies," Momma continued. "Then, the young one dropped us, and we fell into the Big Blue."

The cove creatures were silenced by this second miracle. Hope touched their hearts. If miracles could happen for one, they could happen for all.

Solemnly, the sea creatures came together. Every tuna, crab, dolphin, octopus, stingray, and seahorse looked at the little perch. Even Killer bowed his head.

"Sesom," said Momma Perch, "would you like to call for us?"

Humbly, in a small voice that touched all who heard it, Sesom called with confidence.

"Dear Finmaker," he said. "Thank you for parting the Big Blue to keep us safe."

Remembering the dolphin's question, he added, "Please bring a feast for the Great Whites, so that we can swim together in peace today."

...And to this day, from fish to fish, creature to creature, and ocean to ocean, even the youngest ones know the Legend of the Fire Fish.

Inspired by the historical events
from the book of *Exodus*

"The Prince of Egypt"

*"Do not be afraid. Stand firm and you will see the
deliverance the Lord will bring you, today. "*

Moses

*"Therefore, since we are receiving a kingdom that cannot be
shaken, let us be thankful, and so worship God acceptably
with reverence and awe, for our 'God is a consuming fire.'"*

Hebrews 12:28-29

Jordan's Gift

Every spring, one mother sheep was honored when her newborn lamb was chosen as a living gift by her two-legged master. Always, the honored mother watched her lamb leave with sorrow at parting, but rejoiced that it had been chosen to serve her master. This year, no gift was taken. Curious, a group of mothers journeyed to find out why, only to discover the true meaning of pain, sacrifice, and perfect love.